Batman, aka Bruce Wayne, is a billion
who fights crime in Gotham City. He
intellect, detective skills, and gadgets rather than
superhuman powers.

Deadpool, aka Wade Wilson, can heal really fast from any injury. Deadpool talks to the audience and knows he's in a pretend world, which makes his stories funny and special.

Superman's, aka Clark Kent, real name is Kal-El, and he hails from the planet Krypton. His powers include superhuman strength, flight, and heat vision.

Captain Marvel, aka Carol Danvers, gains superhuman strength, energy projection, and flight powers from an alien Kree source. She is one of the most powerful heroes in the Marvel Universe, capable of cosmic-level feats.

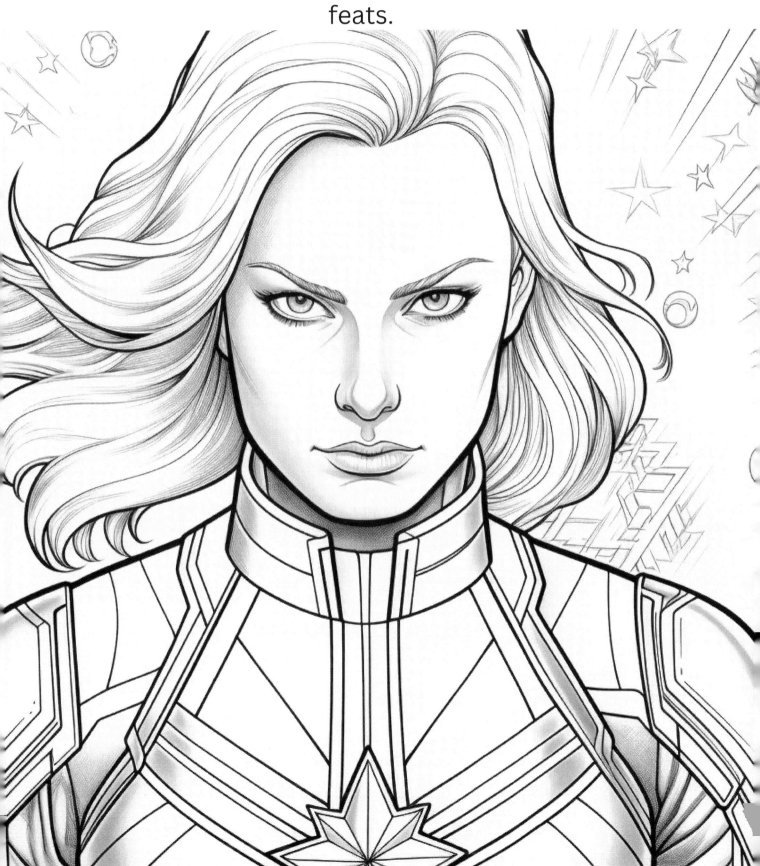

Barry Allen, also known as The Flash, is the fastest man alive, capable of incredible speed and reflexes. He taps into the Speed Force, a cosmic energy source that grants him superhuman velocity.

Scarlet Witch, aka Wanda Maximoff, has amazing magical powers! She can use chaos magic to control reality, create energy blasts, and move objects with her mind. Her powers make her very powerful.

Captain America's real name is Steve Rogers, and he gained his enhanced abilities through a super-soldier serum. He wields a vibranium shield and is known for his sense of justice and leadership.

Dr. Stephen Strange is a skilled surgeon who becomes the Sorcerer Supreme, mastering mystic arts. He wields the Eye of Agamotto, which grants him access to powerful spells and the ability to change time.

Aquaman, also known as Arthur Curry, is the ruler of Atlantis with superhuman strength, aquatic abilities, and the power to communicate with marine life. He wields a legendary trident that represents his royal lineage

Hawkeye is another superhero name for Clint Barton. He's really good at shooting arrows and hitting targets perfectly. He's an important part of the Avengers team and uses special arrows that can do all kinds of cool things!

Black Widow is another name for Natasha Romanoff. She's an amazing spy and fighter! She's really good at sneaking around and using her quick moves to win battles against bad guys.

She-Hulk, whose real name is Jennifer Walters, became a superhero after a blood transfusion from her cousin Bruce Banner (the Hulk). She turns into a big, green, super-strong hero when she gets angry or excited and is also a skilled lawyer fighting for justice.

Ant-Man, whose real name is Scott Lang, is a superhero with incredible powers. He can shrink down to the size of an ant and still have super strength! Not only that, he can communicate with insects, like ants, and they become his little friends, helping him during his exciting adventures.

Wolverine, aka James Howlett or Logan, is a superhero with awesome powers! He can heal really fast from any injury, making him almost invincible. He also has sharp claws made of a strong metal called adamantium, which he uses to fight bad guys and be a fearsome warrior!

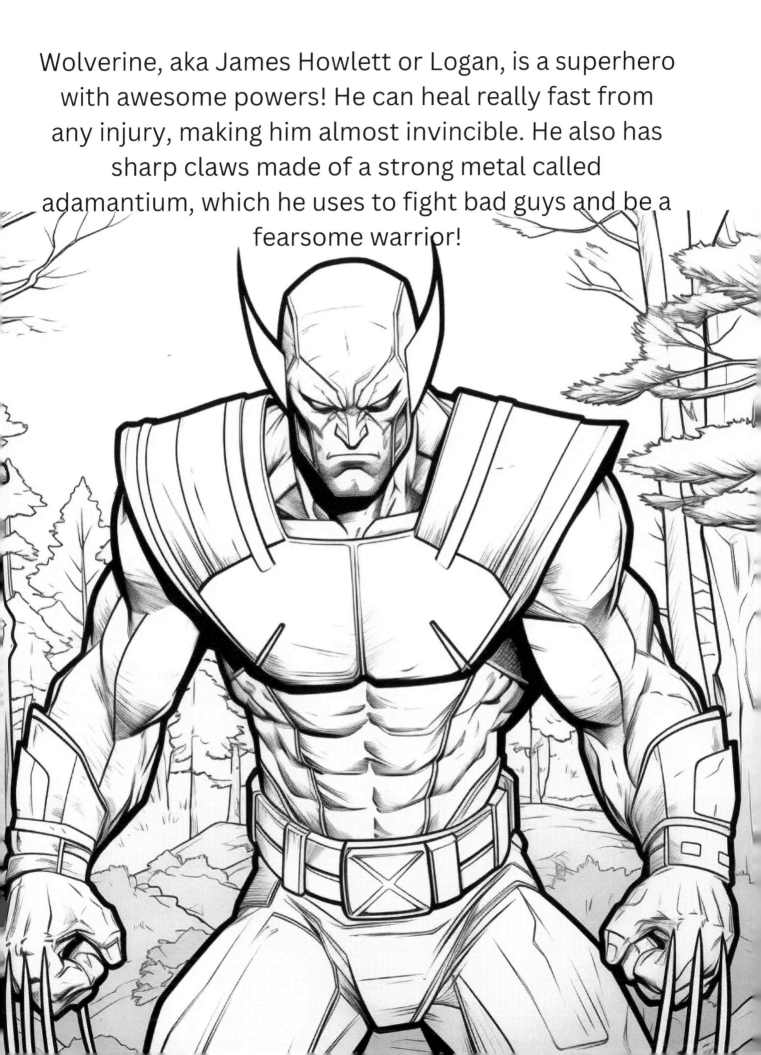

Marvel Falcon, also known as Sam Wilson, is a superhero who can fly with his bird-like wingsuit. He can talk to birds and has a special bird companion named Redwing. Together, they help people and go on exciting adventures!

T'Challa is a powerful king in Wakanda and a superhero called the Black Panther. He has super strength, can move quickly, and has sharp senses. When he fights bad guys, he wears a special suit made of Vibranium that keeps him safe and can absorb energy.

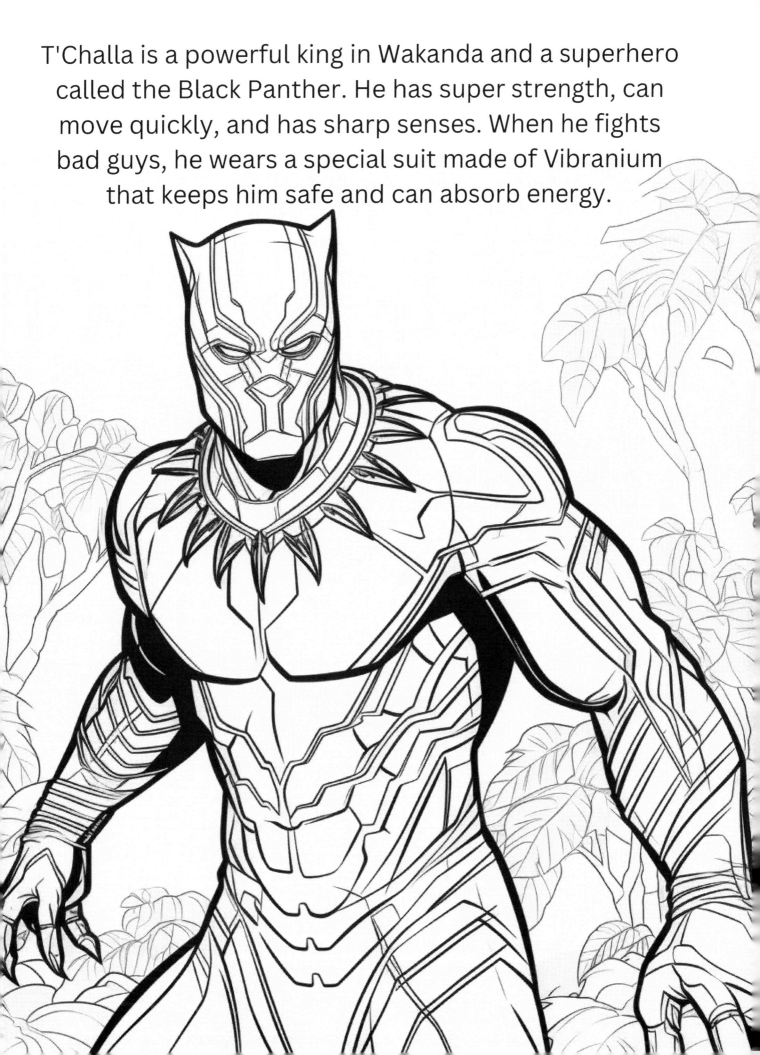

Dr. Bruce Banner is a scientist who turns into the Hulk, a huge green creature, whenever he gets really mad. The angrier he gets, the stronger he becomes! Even if he gets hurt, he can heal and get better quickly.

Spider-Man's real name is Peter Parker, and he's a high school student living in New York City. One day, he got bitten by a special spider that gave him amazing superpowers!

Tony Stark is a super-smart billionaire who made a special suit and became Iron Man. With his suit, he can fly, become super strong, and use all kinds of cool weapons and gadgets!

Wonder Woman is also called Diana Prince, and she's a princess from a special place called Themyscira. She has super strength, can run really fast, and uses a magical lasso that makes people tell the truth!

Thor is a powerful god from Norse mythology, and he controls thunder and lightning. He is really strong too! He uses a magical hammer called Mjolnir, and only those who are worthy can lift it.

Supergirl, whose real name is Kara Zor-El, is Superman's cousin. She has powers just like him and protects the Earth from bad guys. She can shoot heat from her eyes, freeze things with her breath, and has super strength!

Miles Morales is the new Spider-Man, getting his powers from a special spider bite. He has unique abilities like turning invisible and using a "venom sting" to stop villains, making him an awesome hero!

Gwen Stacy is Spider-Woman or Ghost Spider, with powers like swinging from webs and climbing walls. She's a close friend of the original Spider-Man, Peter Parker, and they fight bad guys together. Gwen is a smart and brave hero!

America Chavez, also known as Miss America, is a young superhero with cool superpowers. She can fly through dimensions, travel to different worlds, and has super strength. With her bravery, she fights villains and protects people from harm.

Ms. Marvel, also known as Kamala Khan, is a superhero with stretchy powers. She can make her arms, legs, and even her whole body stretch far. With her unique abilities and strong sense of justice, she fights bad guys and helps people in need!

Batgirl, whose real name is Barbara Gordon, is a superhero with brilliant detective skills. She fights crime alongside Batman and Robin to keep her city safe!

Daredevil, also known as Matt Murdock, the "Man Without Fear." Despite being blind, he has super-strong senses that help him fight crime and protect the city!

Star-Lord, also known as Peter Quill, is a Marvel superhero. He's great with gadgets, like a special space mask and a cool jetpack. With the Guardians of the Galaxy, he protects the universe on exciting adventures!

Ghost Rider, also known as Johnny Blaze, is a superhero with a fiery skull head. He rides a magical motorcycle and uses his powers to fight bad guys and keep the world safe!

Made in United States
Troutdale, OR
04/16/2024

19218193R00035